L. U. Reavis

## The National Capital Movable

A letter to President Grant on the subject of the removal of the national

capital

L. U. Reavis

**The National Capital Movable**
*A letter to President Grant on the subject of the removal of the national capital*

ISBN/EAN: 9783337403539

Printed in Europe, USA, Canada, Australia, Japan

Cover: Foto ©Andreas Hilbeck / pixelio.de

More available books at **www.hansebooks.com**

# THE NATIONAL CAPITAL MOVABLE.

A

# LETTER TO PRESIDENT GRANT

ON THE SUBJECT OF THE REMOVAL

OF THE

# NATIONAL CAPITAL.

## BY L. U. REAVIS.

ST. LOUIS:

MISSOURI DEMOCRAT BOOK AND JOB PRINTING HOUSE.

1871.

# REMOVAL OF THE NATIONAL CAPITAL.

[FROM THE BURLINGTON (IOWA) HAWKEYE.]

" Mr. L. U. Reavis, of St. Louis, addresses a long and exhaustive letter to President Grant on the subject of the removal of the National Capital. The letter is published in the New York *Tribune* of Saturday, occupying between six and seven of the broad columns of that paper, set in small type. If the President reads it — there's the rub — and duly ponders its facts and arguments, it will be safe to say that he will know a good deal more about the matter than the majority of our public men. We hope Mr. R.'s letter may be printed in pamphlet form, and scattered widely over the country. It contains just such facts and suggestions as the people need to form an intelligent judgment relative to the important question."

# THE NATIONAL CAPITAL.

## LETTER TO THE PRESIDENT.

[*From the New York Tribune, January 28, 1871.*]

PRESIDENT GRANT'S REMARKS ON THE REMOVAL OF THE CAPITAL
CONSIDERED — THE ARGUMENT IN FAVOR OF REMOVAL — HISTORY
OF THE CAPITAL QUESTION — OPINIONS OF AMERICAN STATESMEN
— IMPERATIVE DEMAND FOR REMOVAL.

*To His Excellency* ULYSSES S. GRANT,
*President of the United States:*

SIR: The friends of Capital removal would have been content, during the preliminary discussion, with your silence upon
the subject until you deemed it of sufficient importance to give
it your special consideration in an official way. But as you have,
from time to time during the agitation, intimated your marked
friendship for the people of Washington City, and the eternal
retention of the Capital at that place, and manifestly shown
indifference toward the West, especially by your recent official
and individual action in virtual opposition to the removal, it
becomes the imperative duty of the friends of Capital removal
to hold you alike responsible and subject to the same criticism
invoked by those who do not comprehend the magnitude of the
question. I shall therefore assume to call you to account upon
this great subject, so vital to our national life, and arraign you
before the great men of the Republic, both living and dead, who
have stood in different quarters of the country and beheld alike,

with prophetic eyes, the rising glory and greatness of the nation, and foreseen the coming changes in the governmental dominion, and the redistribution of political and material power over the wide domain of the continent.

I shall bring to bear for your consideration an array of facts and arguments bearing directly and indirectly upon this subject, against which no reasonable man will dare attempt an answer.

That the public may be fully advised of the inciting cause that called out this discussion, and that you be reminded of the grounds upon which it is based, I here insert your words as I found them in the dispatches from Washington City, bearing date of December 21, 1870, as follows:

### "WELCOME TO CONGRESS.

"A large number of citizens, including boys in blue and members of the fire department, had a torch-light procession to-night, to give a welcome to Congress. They marched to the Executive mansion, and a committee was met by the President in the vestibule. Judge Barrett addressed the President, saying they came to tender their respects to him, the man whom every true American delighted to honor.

### "PRESIDENT'S SPEECH.

"The President made the following reply: 'I can not thank you appropriately for the honor you have done me in calling on me this cold night, nor would I detain those out-doors to hear a speech, knowing that they are to make calls at other places, and on gentlemen who, no doubt, will thank them in appropriate terms. I will only say it has always been my desire to see this great nation built up in a manner worthy of a great and growing Republic like ours.

"'As to the removal of the Capital, I think it improbable in the extreme; nor do I believe the removal should be subject to a mere majority of the representatives of the people, elected for a single term. I think the question of the removal, if ever presented, should go through the same process, at least, as amendments to the Constitution, even if there is constitutional power to remove it, which is not settled. This language may seem unpopular for a person coming from that part of the country where I belong, but it is nevertheless expressed with earnestness and without reserve.  Gentlemen, I thank you for your attention and kindness.' "

Now, Mr. President, what you think on the subject of the removal of the Capital is simply the expression of an inconsiderate individual opinion.  Is it possible that a man in your official position would express himself so loosely on so great a subject as the one under consideration ?  You say, as to the removal of the Capital, you think it improbable in the extreme.  This expression is unquestioned evidence that you have not weighed the subject in your mind.  Do you think it improbable that the Mississippi is larger than the Potomac ?  Do you think it improbable that Missouri is larger than all the New England States ?  And do you think it improbable that she possesses more valuable resources than they do ? and that the national debt could be dug out of her soil much sooner and in greater abundance than it could be taken from the mountain system of the West, as you declared in your message one year ago?  You say you believe the removal should not be subject to a mere majority of the representatives of the people.  This expression, Mr. President, still more betrays your inconsiderate action on the subject.  Do you forget that this is a government of majorities ; that the popular will of the people expressed in the ballot-box, or by their representatives in Congress, is the governing attribute and law of the nation?  It was for these principles that you so bravely contended on the battle-field, and by the exercise of this principle you were elevated to your present official position.

But it is not my object, Mr. President, to address you with analysis and criticism, but to, vindicate, against your opposition, the cause of Capital removal, by systematic and irrefutable argument, in the following manner :

## I.  THE RIGHT OF DISCUSSION.

The right to discuss all questions relating to the well-being of this people and nation is inherent ; it is a privilege derived from the organic nature of the government, and alike the same in all the States, and to all the people. Standing upon this broad basis of political right, you must know that the subject of the removal of the National Capital is a legitimate subject for the American people to discuss.

## II. THE BASIS OF DISCUSSION.

At the base of the discussion:

1. It is assumed by the friends of Capital removal that the fathers of the country, in the exercise of the power to remove the seat of the general government from New York to its present place, legislated for themselves as they thought best, and selected for the new seat of government a place central to the then existing States of the young Republic. It was their right to legislate for themselves; they did so according to their judgment and their wants.

2. It is assumed by the friends of Capital removal that this people have the same right to legislate for themselves as our fathers had for themselves, and that it is their right to legislate for themselves according to their judgment and their wants, and that the wants of this people, though the same in principle, are not the same in character.

The Capital that was then suited to the wants of an infant nation, born on a narrow strip of land on the shore of the ocean, is not now suited to the wants of a Republic almost embracing an entire continent, and commanding the commerce of the world and the admiration of the nations of the earth.

3. It is assumed by the friends of Capital removal that the seat of government, at its present place, is not adapted to the national life, nor to the wants of our continental people; that, at every stage of the national growth, Washington City is rendered less fit to be the Capital of this nation, and that therefore the Capital ought to be removed to some more central and convenient place in the wide domain of this continental commonwealth.

4. It is assumed by the friends of Capital removal that, inasmuch as this is " a government of the people and by the people and for the people," its Capital ought to be central and convenient to the great majority of the people who are to be its guardians and defenders.

5. It is assumed by·the friends of Capital removal that the center of human power in this nation will be fixed and organized, at an early date, in the center of the productive energies of the country, and that against the truth of this assumption no argument can be made.

In elaboration of the foregoing propositions as the basis of the discussion, your attention·is asked, Mr. President, to the argument of the question.

### III. The Argument.

At the very outset of the presentation of the argument, let me suppose that some opponent to the movement asks, Why do we want the Capital removed? What good will its removal subserve to the general interest of the government? I answer: That the Capital of a nation, in its true relations to government, must serve a double purpose. Not only is it necessary for it to be the seat of the national legislation, but with equal necessity must it be representative in its influence and character upon the nation. All history furnishes evidence of the truth of this position. Scarcely was there a nation of antiquity whose capital was not also its representative city. The middle ages furnish the strongest evidence of this truth in their city States. Where the power is, there is essentially the capital, and it is a universal law that power is essentially central. It is imperfection alone that establishes it outside the center. All laws, human and divine, are at best only means to regulate the action and tendency of man and things ; and if the conventional power' to regulate by legislation is fixed within the influence of the absolute power of control, the reciprocal influence of the one upon the other will be most beneficial to the whole people. This is what the friends of this movement seek to establish in this great Republic, as the greatest fact of its material life.

Akin to this great fact is the important one of locating the seat of government in a republic where it will best subserve the business interests of the people with the government. In a republic like ours, with vast territories unsettled, lands to dispose of, railroads to build, banking and various commercial interests to protect, a vast number of people have business to transact from year to year at the seat of government; and for this, too, it is the right of the people to demand its removal to the central part of the country.

In support of these claims the following facts are offered as testimony:

When the first Congress, sitting at New York in 1790, selected the present site for the national government, the United States, exclusive of the Northwestern Territory, embraced a narrow strip of the Atlantic Slope consisting of an area of 341,756 square miles, and had 3,929,827 inhabitants — scarcely more than the present population of the State of New York. Not a foot of land did our government own beyond the Mississippi, nor did she prize her possessions beyond the Appalachian mountains of much value, for the Indian, the buffalo, the deer, and panther ruled supreme.

In selecting a permanent seat of government, the Congress of 1790 legislated in the special interest of the thirteen original States — legislated exclusively for themselves. This was their wisdom: appropriate and just to themselves and their times, but to us an error. They were a small band of people; we are a continental people. Our national legislation must conform to our wants and our times, and cannot be gauged by the narrow limits of the old government of 1790.

From an area of 610,512 square miles, including the Northwestern Territory, the national domain has grown to an area of 2,950,264 square miles, exclusive of Alaska — more than three times as large as the old government, and embracing within its control the shores of two oceans, the greatest gulf, the mightiest lakes and rivers in the world.

Of the vast domain which now composes our territorial extent, 860,000 square miles lie east of the Mississippi, and 2,070,000 west of it, exclusive of Alaska, which has 577,390 square miles. Thus it will be seen that by the Louisiana purchase in 1800 we acquired more than double the territorial area, and the full control of the great rivers and the inexhaustible mineral wealth of the mountains; and these acquisitions have been made since the location of the Capital at Washington.

## POPULATION.

This is the most interesting and valuable part of the whole argument. As I have already stated, the entire population of our country in 1790, when Washington was made the seat of government, was 3,929,827. In the space of eighty years we have grown to nearly 40,000,000, as our present census will show. Of these, less than 19,000,000 belong to the Atlantic Slope, 19,000,000 to the Mississippi Valley, and at least 2,000,-000 to the Pacific Slope. This will give to the West a preponderance of population.

Of this entire population there will not be an average of fourteen to the square mile of our vast domain, exclusive of Alaska. But, from the rapid increase of our people, may we not look for all these numbers to be swelled far beyond our ordinary conception in the brief space of a lifetime? The increase of population in the Northwest, during the decade between 1850 and 1860, was 67.9 per cent., while the ratio of increase in the whole country was 35.52. The popular vote of 1852 shows the Northwest to have cast 29.46 per cent. of the entire vote. But, aside from any local causes that may have existed to produce a more rapid increase of population in one locality than another, there is an exact law of human development which, when properly applied, solves this problem of population with exact mathematical accuracy. Malthus laid down the law to be this: That the productive power of healthy, well-clad, well-fed, and well-lodged people, was so great that fully two children would be born for every person who died within a given time. Therefore, he fixed thirty-three years as the time necessary for any people to double their number. George Combe, commenting upon the doctrine of Malthus, wrote that in the new States of North America the population doubled every twenty-five years, independent of immigration.

Dr. Elder, a prominent writer on Political Economy in our own land, writes that our population doubles every twenty-three and a half years ; and the recent calculations of our government are based upon twenty-three years as the time necessary for doubling. With these facts before us, what may we not expect to be our increase before the century closes? Taking the calculation of Dr. Elder as being correct, may we not assume that, before the century expires, more than 100,000,000 people will occupy the present area of our country ? And with the increased facilities for immigration, and the rapid development of our resources, the child is now born that will see more than 300,000,- 000 people residing upon our present domain.

Of these, not more than 70,000,000 will inhabit the Atlantic Slope, while more than 230,000,000 will inhabit the interior plain and the region beyond it.

### COMMERCE.

But, Mr. President, let us pass from the subject of population to a consideration of the commerce of the country. And here I must express my regret that I cannot present to you an analysis of the facts which our new census will reveal ; yet I am happy to say that I can make my argument strong without them. The Atlantic seaboard of the United States extends about 3,500 miles, and the Mississippi and its tributaries afford an inland navigation of 30,000 miles, upon the bosom of which now floats an amount of commerce three times as great in value as the whole foreign commerce of the country.          .

In former times our trade with foreign parts was looked upon as our most important interest. It is now dwarfed in comparison by the transportation and handling of domestic produce for domestic markets.

In 1867 the entire products of the United States were $1,900,- 000,000. Its exports were less than one-fifth of this amount, leaving four-fifths to be exchanged between the States. It is said that at the present time not more than one-fifteenth of the business of New York city is based upon foreign commerce.

The Mississippi drains 2,445,000 square miles, which is more than half the number of square miles in the United States. The surface contains 768,000,000 acres of the finest land in the world. It has space for one hundred and fifty States the size of Massachusetts, and, were its population in the same proportion, it would contain more than five times the present population of the whole United States. At this time not more than one acre in five is under cultivation, and the vast resources of coal and minerals have hardly begun to be fairly developed. The value of the commerce of the Mississippi is estimated at $2,000,000; and the Agricultural Bureau, basing its calculations upon past results, estimate that the cereal products of the Northwest will, in 1900, amount to 3,121,970,000 bushels. In addition to these vast statements of wealth, we are enabled to bring in as reinforcements the productions and commerce of the Pacific Slope, which, in itself, has the strength and value of an empire, and far transcends the commerce of the old government of 1790; and in whatsoever manner we examine the commerce of our country, whether interiorly, upon the lakes, adjoining the Gulf, or upon the Pacific Slope, we find the assurance that in either case a few more years will show an equal, if not greater, commerce than the Atlantic Slope can afford.

There are now in the United States more than 50,000 miles of railway, three-fifths of which lie west of the Appalachian mountains, in the Valley States and Pacific Slope. They have been constructed at a cost of about $2,000,000,000; and yet not half of our vast country is supplied with roads. Another twenty-five years will almost double the number of miles already built. In addition to the wonderful system of railways, who can conceive of the mightiness of our future shipping upon the ocean and inland waters, all of which will contribute to swell our national greatness at home and our fame abroad?

### POLITICAL.

There are also political reasons, Mr. President, why the Capital should be removed to the West. The balance of power in the National Legislature has already passed west of the Appalachian mountains, and belongs to the States and Territories lying beyond. And when we consider how great the disproportion will be in the National Legislature when the "New West" is carved into States, we cannot fail to see the justness of the demand for a more central location of the National Capital.

Look at the facts for one moment. The Atlantic Slope has an area of 423,197 square miles, which is divided into seventeen States. Under the Constitution they are all allowed thirty-four

Senators and one hundred and twenty Representatives in the National Legislature. The Mississippi Valley has an area of 2,445,000 square miles, with less than one-third of its territory made into States. It now has eighteen States, which, under the Federal Constitution, are allowed thirty-six Senators and one hundred and fifteen Representatives in the National Legislature. The Pacific Slope has an area of 627,256 square miles, part of which is made into three States, which are entitled to six Senators and five Representatives in the National Legislature. Alaska has an area of 577,390 square miles, and is large enough to make more than fourteen States as large as Ohio. Another view shows 860,000 square miles east of the Mississippi river, which is already divided into twenty-seven States, including Louisiana and West Virginia. These send fifty-four Senators and two hundred and five Representatives to the National Legislature. West of the Mississippi river we have 2,070,000 square miles, exclusive of Alaska, which, at the least calculation, ought to be made into fifty new States, each one of them being larger than Ohio, and containing 40,000 square miles.

Again, the States of the Atlantic Slope have thirty-four Senators and one hundred and twenty Representatives in the National Legislature. The Mississippi Valley, together with the Pacific Slope, has forty-two Senators and one hundred and twenty Representatives; this places the balance of power in the Senate west of the Alleghanies, and makes an equal representation in the House of Representatives. But how long, Mr. President, will this remain the order of political representation in the National Legislature? Not only will the West gain by the apportionment under the new census, but also will new States succeed each other in coming into the Union, as we go forward in our national growth and progress.

But you say, Mr. President, that you are not willing to submit this question to a majority of the representatives of the people. Ah, Mr. President, that was a fatal expression for you to make; the great people all over the country heard you speak the word. Are you to sit in the chair of Washington and dictate terms to the people, which he dared not do, and to object to the people's representatives doing that which is their plain and lawful duty?

Do you claim the right to exercise such unlawful authority ? If you do, let me advise you to reverse your decision, for no power on earth can enforce it. It will prove to be a more heathen declaration than that of Xerxes writing to Mount Athos, and ordering it to get out of the way of his march, or his vain attempt to chain the Hellespont and stay its ebbing waves ; or than that of Mohammed, asking the mountain to come to him ; the sequel showed that Mohammed had to go to the mountain ; and with equal propriety may it be said that the National Capital will and must gravitate to the great center of population.

But, Mr. President, aside from the question of numerical and political power which belongs to the West, and its claims as the center of our territory, there is a paramount necessity for locating the seat of government of the nation in the midst of its material power. The life of a nation is made doubly secure when united with the strongest and greatest commercial and material interests of her people ; for, thus united, they complement each other, and the security and perpetuity of the one becomes the security for the perpetuity of the other. Nothing can be more absurd than to imagine that the life and perpetuity of this Republic is as secure for the future, with the seat of government at Washington — a distant place on the outskirts of the country, with no material power or prestige — as it would be in a central position in the Mississippi Valley, where the great vitalizing heart of the Republic is destined to beat in harmony with its onward progress and greatness.

## IV. Congressional Discussion of the Subject.

Mr. President: Having presented an incontestable array of arguments, facts and figures, to prove an entirely different state of things in the political, commercial, and material character of our country than that which existed at the time of the location of the present Capital, thus proving beyond question the necessity of a change of location, I will now present, as subordinate to the argument, a synopsis of discussions made in Congress, at different times in our country's history, upon the subject of Capital removal. To save unnecessary labor in this matter, I

here quote from a paper prepared from the debates by Mr.
George Alfred Townsend, as follows :

"The main argument of the tradesmen and property-holders
of the village of Washington, for the retention of the Capital
among them, is that this spot was ' consecrated by the preference
of all the patriots.' It is so common for statements of this
kind to be made without authority and circulated through
ignorance, that I recently took opportunity to overhaul the
venerable 'Debates and Proceedings in the Congress of the
United States,' published by Gales & Seaton, as well as the
debates of later Congresses, published by John C. Rives, to see
upon what foundation stood the warrior's pride. And, as I
anticipated, the forefathers approached this subject with the
same practical sagacity which we are called upon to assume in
reconsidering it. They looked for no omens or sacred birds to
fix their choice. They took Washington City as a compromise
against the wish of a majority of them, and particularly against
the wish of the Eastern State and Middle State people and
statesmen. They spoke of the importance of getting as far
westward as possible, as far back as 1789, and they did go as far
West as practicable, considering the narrow strand of population
and the condition of American highways at that time. From
the moment Washington was fixed upon, the common sense of
the East revolted, and a smothered dislike of the site was mani-
fested till 1814, when by three several votes it was resolved to
go to a city further north, and this resolution obtained the vote
of the Speaker of the House of Representatives, Langdon
Cheves, of South Carolina, and the removal was only prevented
by the extraordinary efforts of the people of Washington village,
who built at their own expense a new edifice for Congress—since
called the Old Capitol Prison. After this the discontent con-
tinued, till, in 1846, Alexandria, with more pride than Washington, demanded to be retroceded to Virginia, so that she could
have a self-existent anatomy ; and then the call for a movement
into the Valley of the Mississippi became distinct and decided.
That there may be no mistake in this matter, I append all the
material points of the debates extant, of the three periods
referred to. There is not the remotest indication anywhere that

Washington City would have had a ghost of a chance for being the Capital site ten years after its foundation. Virginia alone kept the seat of Government on the Potomac."

## WASHINGTON SELECTED IN DEFERENCE TO THE WEST.

On the 27th of August, 1789, Congress sitting in New York city, Mr. Scott, of Pennsylvania, introduced the resolution in Congress which provided for a permanent Capital, in these words:

*Resolved*, That a permanent residence ought to be fixed for the general government of the United States at some convenient place, as near the center of wealth, population, and extent of territory, as may be consistent with convenience to the navigation of the Atlantic Ocean, and having due regard to the particular situation of the western country.

The terms of this resolution are almost exactly applicable to the present movement for readjusting "the center of wealth, population, and territory."

Among the few debaters recorded on this proposition were Scott, Jackson of Georgia, Goodhue of Massachusetts, Lee of Virginia, and the illustrious James Madison.

Goodhue "favored the Susquehanna, either at Harrisburg or opposite Havre de Grace."

Jackson said that "upon this subject depended the existence of the Union. The place of the seat of government was important in every point of view. It might be compared to the heart of the human body; it was a center from which the principles of life were carried to the extremities, and from these might return again with precision."

In 1869 Jackson would have found this heart in the extremities, like the bulb in a thermometer.

Scott thought "the principles of the Union were the principles of equal justice and reciprocity. He conceived the question now before the House as grand a link as any in the Federal chain. The future tranquillity of the United States depended as much on this as on any other question that ever had or could come before Congress. It was a justice due to the extremities of the continent to adopt such a measure."

Had Scott so spoken in th    ys he would have been accused,
in the garbage prints o'    hington, of "speculating in St.
Louis corner lots!"

Mr. Lee, of Virginia (Light Horse Harry), said: "A place
as nearly central as a con    ient communication with the Atlantic
Ocean and an easy        o the western territory will permit,
ought to be selected an    blished as the permanent seat of the
government of th    States. Will gentlemen say that the
center of governm    ald not be the center of the Union?
Will they say ou        brethren are to be disregarded? These
are momentous col, ide   tions, which should lead the House to a
conclusion. If they are disregarded it will be an alarming circumstance to the people of the Southern States, who have felt
their alarms already."

This was the same man who delivered over Washington the
funeral eulogy of " First in war, first, in peace, and first in the
hearts of his countrymen." He was Washington's neighbor, and
his argument is directly in the line of the Mississippi Valley.

The entire argument of those urging the Potomac for the site
of the Capital was that it was the highway to the West, and that
the West should be consulted, while the Northern men pressed
the Susquehanna as being the true route westward.

## MADISON ON A NEW CAPITAL SITE.

Perhaps the greatest authority, however, was the illustrious
James Madison, who spoke as follows on September 3, 1789:

"An equal attention to the rights of the community is the
basis of republics. If we consider, Sir, the effects of legislative
power on the aggregate community, we must feel equal induce-
ments to look for the center in order to find the present seat of
Government. Those who are most adjacent to the seat of legislation will always possess advantages over others. An earlier
knowledge of the laws, a greater influence in enacting them, and
a thousand other circumstances, will give a superiority to those
who are thus situated. If we consider the influence of the
Government in its Executive Department, there is no less reason
to conclude that it ought to be placed in the center of the Union.

2

It ought to be in a situation to command information from every part of the Union ; to watch every conjecture; to seize every circumstance that can be improved. The Executive eye ought to be placed where it can best see the dangers which threaten ; and the Executive arm whence it may be extended most effectually to the protection of every part. In the Judiciary Department, if it is not equally necessary, it is highly important that the Government should be equally accessible to all. With respect to the Western territory, we are not now to expect it, for it would be an affront to the understanding of our fellow-citizens of the Western waters, that they will be united with their Atlantic brethren on any principle than that of equality and justice. We had every inducement, both of interest and prudence, to fix on the Potomac as most satisfactory to our Western brethren. He defied any gentleman to cast his eye, in the most cursory manner, over a map and say that the Potomac is not much nearer this center than any part of the Susquehanna. He granted that the present center of population is nearer the Susquehanna than the Potomac. But are we choosing a seat of Government for the present moment only ? He presumed not !"

This speech was quoted in 1846 in favor of the removal of the Capital to the Ohio, by Mr. Pennybacker, in Congress. There is not a word in it which does not justify and encourage the present movement for a new Capital city in the great Western Valley. A Committee of seven were appointed to select a central site, by a vote of only 72 to 71 ; and at the head of this Committee was Mr. Fisk, of New York.

### THE REMOVAL AGITATION IN 1814.

On the 26th of December, 1814, Mr. Fisk, of New York, rose in the House and introduced the following resolution :

"*Resolved*, That a Committee be appointed to inquire into the expediency of removing the seat of Government during the present session of Congress, to a place of greater security and less inconvenience than the City of Washington, with leave to report by bill or otherwise."

By a vote of 79 to 37 the resolution was taken into immediate consideration, and debated till October 15. At this time the

Capitol wings were in ashes, and Congress met in the unfinished Patent Office. I append the material extracts from the debates.

Mr. Fisk, of New York — "Where shall Congress sit with safety and convenience? Some designate one place, some another; but few imagine that the councils of the nation will continue here. The confidence and the credit of the nation is identified with the security of the public councils and the safety of the public records."

Mr. Lewis, of Virginia — "A temporary removal only is contemplated; but once started, the Capital will never return. For the last ten or twelve years similar attempts have been made."

Mr. Fisk, of New York — "On a removal to any other place, the inconveniences of this would appear by contrast so strongly that the Government could never be induced to return."

Mr. Grosvenor, of New York — "The gentleman from South Carolina conceives that a removal will be striking our colors. 'Wait,' says that gentleman, 'till the enemy comes and chases you off.' That is the very dishonor I dread from remaining — the very disgrace I wish to avoid. The gentleman from Tennessee says if his house was burned he would not move off his farm. But suppose a neighbor would politely offer him a clean bed and excellent food and accommodations, would he refuse the use of them and rather sleep in his barn? Let gentlemen ask themselves fairly, Were they willing to appropriate the money of the people of the United States to build a Capitol where it might be destroyed in twenty days? Let them remove to a place of safety, where it would not be necessary to expend $10,000,000 or $15,000,000, or any other sum, for the simple defense of Congress."

Mr. Oakley, of New York — "It was owing to the forbearance of the British that Congress had now a single roof to cover their heads. They had been told that this place was defensible up to the moment when the enemy arrived. Immediately afterward another city on the Atlantic coast had been attacked. Whatever respect he might feel for the inhabitants of this District, their interests could not for a moment enter into competition with the interests of the nation."

Mr. Hansow, of Maryland, "entertained very great contempt for the people of Washington."

The Speaker, Langdon Cheves, S. C., said: "This District cannot be defended, except at immense expense — an expense, perhaps, half that required to carry on the war."

Richard Stockton, of New Jersey, made his maiden speech in favor of removal, October 5, 1814. He said: "Gentlemen had only to look around to survey the District to judge correctly. A permanent seat of government is not required by the Constitution. A power to fix the seat of government for centuries — forever — who can believe that the people of the United States would have invested such a power in the Congress of 1789?— a power to fix a permanent seat of government, without regard to the alterations, improvements, resolutions, and changes which would naturally be produced by a good government, an increasing population, and the settlement of the vast regions of the western country. No, Sir. The great Washington landlord was not to be compensated because he converted barren land into city lots, and made a fortune out of his sales. Was he to be compensated because he was prevented from making more? The speculator, too, must abide by his loss. The government minion was not to be paid for being torn from his hold! The people of this District were entitled to no more than the same kind of defense afforded to their fellow-citizens. The removal of the Capital ought to be decided on principles exclusively public. He had made up his mind, with reluctance, that a removal was essential to the honor and interest of the nation. The dispersion and capture of the members of Congress would gratify the pride and resentment of the English nation more than any other operations their army on the coast could perform. The Military Committee estimated that 20,000 men, costing $30,000 a day, could defend the Capital. The people of the country would not stand this one month, one week, or one day!"

### OTHER VOICES OF 1814.

Mr. Pearson, of North Carolina, said at the same time: "From the first moment we met here we have found almost every member north of Maryland, and a few of the hardy sons of the West, apparently dissatisfied with their accommodations."

Mr. Grosvenor, of New York, alluded to the disposition of the friends of the District to kill the bill by forcing a vote upon it in empty session, and said: "Until the permanence of this site be decided by a full vote, there is not one citizen who ought to have confidence in Washington City. Gentlemen ought to deal liberally, and let the business take the usual course; otherwise, perpetual agitation would ensue."

Mr. Fisk, of New York, said that "we were now 400 miles from the most important seat of war, and the cost of daily and expeditious communication with the lake frontier amounted to a greater sum than the removal of the public offices. To have all these inconveniences merely in consideration of the interests of the people of this District, would be perverting the constitutional principle which gives Congress exclusive legislation over this District, and, instead of that, would be giving the District control over Congress."

Mr. Wright, of Maryland, was not willing any longer to suspend the people of this city by their eyelids. He hoped they would come to a speedy and eternal decision.

Among those who voted for removal were Daniel Webster, Mr. Alston of North Carolina, Ezra Butler, Ingersoll of Pennsylvania, Kent of New York, Cyrus King of Massachusetts, Timothy Pickering, John Reed, and Richard Stockton.

### RETROCESSION OF ALEXANDRIA.

Another strong demonstration of the state of feeling on this subject was exhibited on the 8th of May, 1846, and at various sessions before and subsequent to that time and the date of the retrocession of Alexandria. It was on this question that the voice of the West was first heard for removal. Senator William Allen, on July 2, said:

"The location of the seat of Government on the Eastern seaboard gave the commercial cities a preponderating influence in the councils of the United States—five hundred-fold to one over the same number of people in the vast interior. They had no Committees from the banks of the Missouri, or even the Ohio. 'lobbying' in these halls to regulate tariff duties. No; they had no association in those Western regions, and delegates to the Capital with the view of obtaining laws to meet the views of individual and sectional interests, instead of the wants and the wishes of the great men of the nation. Fifteen hours before a bill was introduced into Congress, Wall street had knowledge of it, and a delegation was on hand to regulate the details of the bill. Thus had their tariffs been formed; thus the commercial interest overruled all others. The great men of the people lived on the soil—four-fifths of them—and it was in the center that the seat of Government should be located. The Alexandrians seem to have had no fear of losing the Capital."

Robert M. T. Hunter, of Virginia, "spoke of the importance of the retrocession to the people of Alexandria, and depicted in glowing colors the blight that had fallen on that city by reason of her dependence on the General Government; her declining commerce; her premature decay; the desolation which had come upon her, not by the scourge of God, but by the hands of man."

Mr. Bayley, of Accomac, Va., "asked Congress to decide the question of retrocession upon its own merits, with reference solely to national considerations, and without any sort of reference to the local interests or influence of Virginia."

John A. McClernand, of Illinois, said that Congress had full power to change the location of seat of Government, and, in that case, by the operation of law, the District, including territory and people, would revert to the State ceding it.

W. W. Payne, of Alabama, "objected to the bill because we had paid a very large amount of money for the portion of the District of Columbia south of the river Potomac. Was it contemplated to refund this money—not less than $1,000,000? The true object of this bill was to saddle the debt of the corporation of Alexandria upon Congress—another $1,000,000."

Finally, the old Missouri Trojan expressed himself upon the Washington Monument question—a similar scheme to the big Fair first projected here by sundry plumbers and newspaper carriers.

Mr. Thomas II. Benton, in the Senate, January 8, 1848, said: " I am entirely opposed to any action by which an association of individuals can lay hold of the name of the United States for the purpose of going abroad to levy contributions on the human race. If individuals assume to erect a monument, let them do it as individuals, but let no opportunity be afforded them of using the name of the Congress of the United States in furtherance of their individual schemes."

Thus stands history on the removal of the Capital. The voice of self-sacrificing patriotism calls us to look for the center of population, present and to come; to cease expending money on the verge of the East, but to " build deep and strong the everlasting Jerusalem, upon the bank of humanity's Jordan — the river of the Mississippi Valley."

Mr. President, I would ask your especial attention to the soundness of the argument made by Mr. Madison, and how nearly like it have the friends of Capital removal in the recent discussions made their arguments.

V.  THE CONSTITUTIONALITY OF REMOVAL.

But are you ready to say, Mr. President, that although the argument is good, there is a constitutional question in the way? Well, I am not a constitutional lawyer, and therefore cannot discuss the constitutionality of the question; but I will venture to submit to you a few plain facts, which take precedence over all technical objections. Referring to the " Federalist," I find the Constitution of the United States, as agreed on in Convention, September 17, 1787, and which was adopted September 18, 1788, contains the following clause:

Article I, under section 8: " That Congress shall have power to exercise exclusive legislation in all cases whatsoever over such District, not exceeding ten miles square, as may, by cession of particular States and the acceptance of Congress, become the seat of Government of the United States, and to exercise like authority over all places purchased by the consent of the Legislature of the State in which the same shall be, for the erection of forts, magazines, arsenals, dock-yards, and other needful buildings."

Now, Mr. President, I wish you to bear in mind that the above is the only clause in the Constitution touching the subject of the seat of government, and that, while the Constitution was adopted September 13, 1788, the bill for the removal of the Capital from New York to its present place was passed July 9, 1790, by the first Congress during its second session. Now, Sir, I hold it to be true that the Constitution was framed and adopted without any possible reference to a special and permanent location of the seat of government. In fact, several efforts were made, before and after the adoption of the Constitution, to secure the Capital at different places. Congress sat a while at Philadelphia, then at Princeton, New Jersey, from thence adjourned to Annapolis. In October, 1783, it was resolved that buildings for the use of Congress should be erected on the banks of the Delaware. A few days later a resolution was offered that buildings for a similar purpose should be erected on the Potomac, some members conceiving that there was no way to settle the question but to have two Capitals. Again, in the debates upon the bill which resulted in the location of the Capital at its present place, some members desired its permanent location. Mr. Madison replied to such: "It is not in our power to guard against a repeal. Our acts are not like those of the Medes and Persians, unalterable; a repeal is a thing against which no provision can be made."

Again, those who pretend to believe in a constitutional prohibition couple with their argument the cession of the District of Columbia as the foundation of their faith. Now, what are the facts about that? Was not the Virginia portion of the District of Columbia re-ceded by Congress to the mother State in 1846? Was that act unconstitutional? Was President Polk's proclamation, declaring the retrocession to Virginia, unconstitutional? Did not John C. Calhoun say, in the debate on the subject, that "according to his judgment there could not be any constitutional objection, unless there was somewhere in the Constitution a prohibitory clause? It was in the power of the government to remove its seat if it thought proper, unless there was some express provision to the contrary. Now, he saw no such provision in the Constitution. It belonged to the gentlemen to prove that the retrocession would be unconstitutional. If they had a right, which he held to be incontestable, to remove the seat of government, the right of parting with any portion of it was apparent. The act of Congress, it was true, established this as the permanent seat of government; but they all knew that an act of Congress possessed no perpetuity of obligation."

The Hon. Reverdy Johnson, also being a member of the Senate from Maryland, took part in the discussion on retrocession. He went into a review on the constitutional provision relative to the establishment of a seat of government, and to the proceedings of Congress with regard to its location within the District, and insisted that there was nothing in either to prohibit the retrocession of the ten miles square to the State from which it was taken, or any portion thereof. He supposed that an absolute necessity might arise for the removal of the seat of government, from the possession of the District by an enemy. Mr. Benton held that the question with him was, whether the people of Alexandria were willing to have the territory re-ceded. The constitutionality involved in the question was finally settled by the passage of the bill and the consequent retrocession. That act of itself ought to be sufficient to settle the constitutionality of the question, and prevent any further foolish cavil upon the subject. No, Mr. President, there is no constitutional obstacle in the way. The Constitution is no more in the way of removing the Capital than it is in the way of removing forts, magazines, arsenals, dock-yards, and other needful government buildings. Let no intriguing Washington politician deceive you by the whisperings of a corrupt heart and a weak understanding. Believing, Mr. President, I have fully answered this ill-considered objection, I will pass on to a consideration of the proper place for the Capital.

VI. THE PROPER PLACE FOR THE CAPITAL, AND THE REASONS WHY.

1. I lay it down as a law of civilization that human power in any well-regulated government is developed and organized to its greatest capacity in the midst of the productive energies of the country over which the government extends.

2. I lay it down as an axiomatic truth that in a constitutional or representative government, where all the power is in the people,

its exercise by the majority inheres in them from the very nature of the government.

In support of these two fundamental propositions I offer all the facts in the geology, the topography, and the climate of our country, as well as all our political and material facts and the rapid tendency of our national growth and civilization, and hold that they all evidence the *justness* and the *prime necessity* of a central location for the National Capital. The new Capital should be located in a place the most convenient and the most accessible to all the citizens of the United States, and the most secure against foreign invasion and domestic insurrection.

Midway in the Valley of the Mississippi, between the two great oceans, the future center of the commerce, manufactures, mineral resources, population, productions, and wealth of this continent can only be found. The geological strata, the configuration, the topography, and the isothermal lines of North America show that the center of the Mississippi basin is the place already designated by nature as the future seat of a national Government which now controls and will embrace the continent.

The Capital of a Government which embraces a continent must itself be continental, attesting the magnitude of the power it represents by its own greatness, and by its influence radiating from the center to the remotest circumference.

The old Capital at New York was removed to Washington in 1790, as a place more central to the old colonial States (on the margin of the Atlantic seaboard), and the Capital ought to be removed now for the same reasons that existed then, so as to fix it finally in the present center of the old and new States, in the Valley of the Mississippi, which is as central to the continent as it is to the Republic of the United States. No future acquisitions of territory on this continent could affect the centrality of a Capital located in the middle of the Valley of the Mississippi.

The rapid increase of commerce, of manufactures, of agricultural products, of mineral developments, and of population demonstrate that in a few years this valley, with its tributaries, will contain two-thirds of the population and develop three-fourths of the productions of the United States and Territories ;

and in fifty years from to-day, upon the ratio of increase for the last half century, it will contain about eight-tenths of all the population and wealth of the nation. As the natural center of the population and wealth of the nation, it is the fit and necessary seat of the political center of the Government, where the people and the Government are necessarily brought in daily contact for the common benefit of both. The Creator has placed the heart in the center of our bodies for the perfection of the circulation of the blood, whose functions it is to vitalize and warm our systems ; and so a political seat of a representative system like ours should be located at the heart of the country, where the ebb and flow of the tides and currents of political opinion will traverse the most direct route from the center to the extremities and back again. Such a central location of a political power of a representative government will do much to preserve the nation against all forms of anarchy or despotism. The great political considerations point to the establishment of a central national capital as one of the necessary safeguards for the preservation of a representative form of government.

The present Capital of the nation is more remote from the Pacific States and Territories than Constantinople is from Great Britain, or St. Petersburg from Spain or Morocco.

## VII. PROPHETIC TESTIMONY.

Mr. President: To aid the argument and to strengthen the whole facts which I have thus far presented for your consideration, I desire to call your attention to the prophetic testimony in support of the position of the friends of Capital removal on this question. This part of the subject should properly begin with Plato, and come down through the idealistic minds of intervening ages ; but, for brevity, I will refer you to the Hon. Charles Sumner's Prophetic Voices about America, in the *Atlantic Monthly* of September, 1867, where you will find a vast array of prophetic testimony in favor of the future empire of the American continent. The testimony given in the last half century bears more directly upon the question under consideration, and therefore is in a great measure submitted as follows :

Looking beyond to the future growth of our Continental Government, Henry Clay said, in a speech made in the United States Senate, January, 1824, on the extension of the Cumberland road, and replying to the opposition of Eastern members to Western improvements: "Not to-day, nor to-morrow; but this Government is to last, I trust, forever; we may, at least, hope it will endure until the wave of population, cultivation, and intelligence shall have washed the Rocky Mountains and mingled with the Pacific. Yes, Sir, it is a subject of peculiar delight to me to look forward to the proud and happy period when circulation and association between the Atlantic and the Pacific and the Mexican Gulf shall be free and perfect as things are at this moment in England."

In a speech made by Thomas H. Benton in the United States Senate, March 1, 1825, on the occupation of the Oregon river, he said: "Within a century from this day a population greater than that of the present United States will exist on the west side of the Rocky Mountains. I do not deal in paradoxes, but in propositions as easily demonstrated as the problems of Euclid. Here, then, is the demonstration: Divide one portion of this continent into five equal parts, and there will be found, in the Valley of the Mississippi, three parts; on the east side of the Alleghany Mountains, one part; on the west of the Rocky Mountains, one part. Population will distribute itself accordingly three parts in the valley, and one part on each of the appurtenant slopes.

Within a century the population of the whole will be 160,-000,000, of which 100,000,000 will drink the waters which flow into the Mississippi, and 60,000,000 will be found upon the lateral streams which flow east and west, toward the rising and the setting sun. The calculation is reducible to mathematical precision. We double our numbers once in twenty-five years, and must continue to do so until the action of the prolific principle in man shall be checked by the same cause which checks it in every race of animals—the stint of food. This cannot happen with us until every acre of our generous soil shall be put in requisition ; until the product of more than 1,000,000,000 of acres shall be insufficient to fill the mouths which feed upon them. This will

require more people than a century can produce, even at the rate
doubling once in twenty-five years—a rate which will give us
160,000,000 in the year 1920; that is to say, 20,000,000 more
than the Roman Empire contained in the time of Augustus
Cæsar. A century is but a point in the age of a nation. The
life of an individual often spans it; and many are the children
now born who will see the year 1920, and the accomplishment of
the great events which their nurses believe to be impossible."

The great Webster said in a speech in the Senate on the compromise measures, January 25, 1850: "Sir, nobody can look
over the face of this country at the present moment, nobody can
see where its population is the most dense and growing, without
being made to admit, and compelled to admit, that ere long the
strength of America will be in the Valley of the Mississippi."

Said the Hon. Horace Greeley, in speaking of the West:
"Let her not be despised! American Orientals may dream that
wisdom has taken up her perpetual abode on the shores of the
Atlantic, and that the genii of Art, of Science, of Literature,
have planted their rosy grottoes on the sunny side of the Alleghanies; but a thousand fancies never made one fact. Like the
swaddled Hercules, the West has already put out her infant arms
and strangled two political dragons that were coiling about her
cradle; and as soon as she walks forth in the consciousness of
matured strength, she will make a greater fluttering among the
harpies that prey upon her interests than did the club of the
hero among the Stymphalian vultures. Ill-founded contempt
is a blow that always rebounds. The Assyrian contemned
the Persians, while the Persians, like muskrats, were under-
mining the walls of Babylon. Haughty, learned, philosophic
Greece, the conqueror of Xerxes, became a Turkish slave, and
the fair daughters of Themistocles and Leonidas were bought
and sold in the shambles of Smyrna. Rome despised the barbarians, and the barbarians conquered Rome. Cæsar overran
Gaul with victorious legions, and now Gaul holds a standing
army in the city of the Cæsars. England would force America
to drink Bohea, and America poured out for England a cup of
gunpowder tea, the taste of which she has not yet got out of her
mouth. Thus it is, Arms and Arts, in their onward progress,

have always pitched their tents near the setting sun, and the
conquests of the one and the triumphs of the other have left
fruits to ripen and decay on the track. The very relics of the
ancient empires are now to be dug out of the soil. Civilization,
like the ostrich in its flight, throws sand upon everything behind
her; and before many cycles shall have completed their rounds;
sentimental pilgrims from the humming cities of the Pacific
coast will be seen where Boston, Philadelphia, and New York
now stand, viewing in moonlight contemplation, with the melan-
choly owl, traces of the Athens, the Carthage, and the Babel of
the Western Hemisphere."

At a later date, said the Hon. Charles Sumner:  "The Mississippi Valley speaks for itself as no man can speak. Give us
peace, and population will increase beyond all experience; resources of all kinds will multiply indefinitely; arts will embellish
the land with immortal beauty; the name of Republic will be
exalted until every neighbor, yielding to irresistible attraction,
will seek a new life in becoming a part of the great whole, and
the national example will be more puissant than army or navy for
the conquest of the world."

Said John Bright, the great English statesman, in speaking of
the American Republic, its future greatness and grandeur:  "I
see one vast confederation, stretching from the frozen North in
one unbroken line to the glowing South, and from the wild bil-
lows of the Atlantic, westward, to the calmer waters of the
Pacific; and I see one people, and one law, and one language,
and one faith, and over all that vast Continent the home of freedom and refuge for the oppressed of every race and every clime."

The great field of the West—"As the center of population
and power is to be in the Mississippi Valley in the future, so
must we look thither for the New Man who is to be the redeemer
of our race and character. The Western man already shows
larger, broader, and healthier development, spiritually speaking,
than his brother in the East. He has never been cramped as yet
by any of the restraining forms of social ecclesiasticism; his
mind, like his eye, ranges over large extents, and is not content
to sit down with itself after having acquired a little power over
its fellows. As the Great West is bound to supply laws and

men for the vast future of this continental country, so will it
furnish the religion, whose all-embracing forms are to invite the
entire people into the simple secrets of its worship."

The Men of the West—"One who has not visited the West
knows but little or nothing of the spirit of the Western men.
There is an all-pervading zeal, energy, ambition, push-go-ahead,
seen nowhere else. The blood of the Western man courses more
rapidly in his veins than in the Eastern man or in the European ;
and he thinks, talks, and acts on a larger scale. The Western
farmer wastes more in a year than the Eastern farmer saves.
He may lack refinement, but he has a generous heart for his
friends and a deal of pluck for his enemies. His religion is less
sectarian, less bigoted, and more broad, catholic, and truly
Christian.

Having submitted only a fragment of the strong but direct
prophetic testimony in favor of the future empire of the great
West, and the consequent demand for the Seat of Government, I
now desire to call your attention to some testimony bearing
immediately upon the question of removal.

Since the days of Jefferson, far-seeing men have from time to
time declared that the Capital of the nation would some day be
removed from the Potomac to the Mississippi. At a dinner
given to Mr. Jefferson, in Frederickstown, Md., in honor of the
Louisiana purchase, a gentleman, whose name, I regret, is lost,
while voluntarily defending Mr. Jefferson, against the silly slurs
made about his purchase, said to the guests, as he unrolled the
plat of a grant of land twenty-five miles square, including the
site of Alton, Illinois: "You need not laugh at Mr. Jefferson,
for some day," pointing at his map, "the Capital of the United
States will be located upon this land." The laugh for the moment was turned upon the stranger, and the inquiry made, how
could people ever get there?

The stranger answered, "I don't know, but I think they will
go there by steam." This occurred about 1804, long before
railroads were constructed, even in the very infancy of the
Republic. All along the line of our historic march have men
declared the coming transfer of power from the Atlantic seaboard to the States west of the Alleghanies. In our own time

thousands of the wisest men have declared the removal of the Capital to be inevitable. Said the Hon. Wm. H. Seward, in a political speech at St. Paul in 1860: " The power of the Republic is being gathered in the Mississippi Valley, and with that power will come the Capital of the country."

Said the Hon. Charles Sumner: " I have no love for Washington, and the removal of the Capital is only a question of time."

Said Dr. Draper, in speaking of the Capital at Washington: " It has ceased to be the appropriate, site for the metropolis of the continental Republic. Western influence predominating will draw the Capital into the Mississippi Valley, in absolute security from all foreign attack, and territorially central."

Said the Hon. Richard Yates: " Now, Sir, when I see this country, when I see its vastness and its almost illimitable extent ; when I see the keen eye of capital and business fastened with steady, interested gaze upon the trade of the West, and all our Eastern cities in hot rivalry are reaching out their iron arms to secure our trade ; when I see the railroads that are centering here in St. Louis ; when I see this city, with 60,000 miles of railroad communication and 100,000 miles of telegraphic communication ; when I see that she stands at the headwaters of navigation, extending to the north 3,000 miles and to the south 2,000 miles ; and when I see that she stands in the center of the continent, as it were ; when I see the population moving to the West in vast numbers ; when I see emigration rolling toward the Pacific, and all through these temperate climes I hear the tramp of the iron horse on his way to the Pacific Ocean ; when I see towns and villages springing up in every direction ; when I see States forming into existence, until the city of St. Louis becomes the center as it were of a hundred States, the center of the population and the commerce of this country—when I see all this, Sir, I feel convinced that the seat of empire is to come this side of the Alleghanies, and why may not St. Louis be the future Capital of the United States ?"

Said the Hon. Horace Greeley: " Washington seems to me an unfortunate location for our national metropolis, and sure to be rendered less acceptable by the march of events. Our Capi-

tal should be a great city.  I prefer our greatest city, supporting
a perfectly independent press, whereby all the acts and leanings
of the Government would be criticised with absolute freedom
from deflection in the hope of Federal patronage or the fear of
its withdrawal.  It should be surrounded by a dense, intelligent,
spirited population, readily rallied in myriads to the defense of
the national archives and treasures.  It should be a focus of art,
and literature, and refinement, thus inviting the presence and
commanding the admiration of the choice spirits of the entire
civilized world.  I judge New York to be pre-eminently that
city.  I am quite sure that Washington is not.  Let the subject
be thoughtfully and generally canvassed, and I feel confident
that a change will be approved and demanded.''

Under this head, Mr. President, I could quote to you the great
majority of the ablest newspapers and public men of the country
who are decided for the removal—men and newspapers that are
not depending on a little Government patronage or Washington
flattery for their bread and butter and social and political standing—but I think the testimony sufficient, and hold that if you
have been observant at all upon the tendency of the people upon
this question you must know what the final decision will be.  I
therefore pass on to consider the unfitness of Washington.

VIII.  THE UNFITNESS OF WASHINGTON FOR THE CAPITAL OF
THIS GREAT NATION.

It is assumed, Mr. President, by the friends of Capital removal, that the seat of Government at its present place is not
adapted to the national life, nor to the wants of our continental
people ; that at every stage of the national growth Washington
City is rendered less and less fit to be the Capital of this nation,
and that, therefore, the Capital ought to be removed to some
more central and convenient place in the wide domain of this
continental commonwealth.

No reasonable person would think of confining the full-grown
man to the cradle of his infancy, but would urge him forth to
the chamber and drawing-room suited to his manhood.  So, too,
of this Republic.  The Capital that was once central to the
3

nation—central to the States of the Atlantic slope, and adapted to the wants of an infant people, has, in the multiplication of States to imperial Republic, left the Capital of its infancy on its outskirts, like a barren rock upon a desert shore. The Republic has grown to the West in magnitude and mightiness, until it now embraces the shores of an ocean greater than that upon which it was born ; and in every conceivable view we can take of the subject, Washington appears unfit to remain the Capital of this great nation, and is only a sink-hole for demagogues, hirelings, dependents, politicians, and office-seekers. Horace Greeley once said to me that there was not a heathen city in the world as corrupt as Washington. In fact, Mr. President, all arguments turn upon the unfitness of Washington to be the Capital of the nation, and the fitness of some central place in the great Valley to be the future home of the Government.

Let us look for one moment at this. Ask the statesman for the philosophy of the integrity of government. He will tell you that it must be representative in all its relations to civilization and the great wants of man. Ask the moral philosopher for the philosophy of the integrity of civilization. He will tell you it, too, must be representative in its relations to government and the great interests of man. Now, in the name of heaven, Mr. President, is Washington City in any conceivable way representative of any of the interests of this great nation and people? Not at all. It is the cradle, the home of the infant Republic, which was found in the bulrushes, but now is deliverer and benefactor ; Washington possesses no representative element either in character or locality. No commerce, no industry, no material power, no prestige, no nothing in common with the great representative, political, material, industrial, and progressive interests of this nation. Of the 50,000 miles of railroads in the country, stretching from ocean to ocean, and from the Lakes to the Gulf, she has only one. Her commerce is not equal to that of the meanest port on the coast of Africa. There is not published in the city—in the capital of the great Republic— a newspaper entitled to any consideration. They are all craven, toadying, and distempered papers. Col. Forney endeavors to publish a Court Journal—the *Chronicle*—an organ for the purpose of narrating from day to day all the toady doings of the so-called fashionable suppers, and dinners, and kissing parties &c., &c. When these things are so, Mr. President, is it not possible for you to rise to the dignity of your position—high up in the sphere of clear conception, and behold Washington as Jesus beheld Jerusalem, the city that killed the prophets and stoned them that were sent unto it. " Oh, venal city! if a purchaser could be found thou art gone." But why are these things so ? I answer, it is in the very nature of things, it is in the philosophy of the integrity of a representative government, that its Capital must, in order to subserve its highest purpose, be inseparably identified with the great representative interests of the nation, the symbol of whose power it is. Civilization and government must act in reciprocal relations. Washington has become totally unfit for the Capital of this vast Continental Republic, because it embodies no representative interests common to the people of this great nation. While the Capital is at its present place, the Government, as represented by the law-makers, the administrators of the law, and the officiating officers, has none of the strength of the nation, none of its great vitalizing power and the public interests of the great people to lean upon, to draw vitality from. In the mighty growth of the Republic the nation is essentially left, at Washington, like a lone child forsaken on a desert rock. It grows weak and forgets the great world around it ; it yields to temptations and becomes demoralized.

I speak to you, Mr. President, " the words of truth and soberness," and I say that the Capital *must* be removed from Washington, as a necessity to the HIGHER LIFE of the Republic, and if you don't rise to the grandeur of the occasion, you will be left to the folly of your decision. There is still another reason for removing it which no power in the world can ignore. I refer to a demand which the rising millions of this great valley will soon make for the Capital. A giant empire is now growing up here in the West, soon to be more powerful in peace than the mightiest nation known to history, and from it a voice will go forth of commanding power. It will speak in majorities, and its will must be obeyed. It will be as a great *giant* ruling a continent. Its veins will be coursed by blood from every land. Its arms of

power will extend—one to the Atlantic, the other to the Pacific—
giving parental protection to the children of the nation upon the
shores of the Eastern and Western Oceans. Let me remind you,
Mr. President, that those in power must prepare to hear the voice
of this growing empire of the West, and to obey its will when
it speaks in majorities.

## IX. Objections Answered.

Mr. President, thus far in the discussion by the people at large,
but two objections that have the least possible weight have been
urged against removal.

1. The expense consequent on the change. This objection is
trifling in the extreme, and certainly would not be urged by a
sensible man when familiar with the facts.

The Government owns, in the District of Columbia, 578 acres,
divided into lots, parks, etc. This land was valued in 1868 at
$13,412,293.26. The improvements on the land, including all
the Government expenditures in the whole District for eighty years,
amounted, June 30, 1868, to only $37,390,853.08. Now, Sir,
the man's soul is small and sordid, indeed, who, in the face of
these facts, will contend for one moment that the expense consequent upon the removal is an obstacle. I will venture to say that,
if the opportunity was afforded, Missouri, and, I think, Illinois,
Iowa, Indiana, Ohio, or Kentucky, would incur a debt of $50,-
000,000 if necessary to secure the Capital upon the respective
soil of either; but the work is too great for this mighty nation to
dicker about. It is beneath the dignity of the Republic to consider any proposition beyond the simple cession by a State of a
new District, wherein to place the seat of Government.

2. Another silly objection urged by some, is that the time has
not come for the removal. The present Capital fails to subserve
the present wants of the Government, and is destined to be rendered "less and less acceptable by the march of events," and its
removal to some more central and appropriate place cannot in the
least adversely affect the general good of the country, and therefore the time has come for the removal. I dismiss this objection
as one of no weight whatever.

There still remains, Mr. President, to be considered in connection with the National Capital a conviction, with many, so absurd that it deserves only to be noticed that it may be rendered contemptible. I refer to the conviction that the presence of the Capital at any place tends to demoralize the people and exercise an injurious influence upon the public interests where it may be. I am aware, Mr. President, that you believe in this absurdity. I have been informed that you so expressed yourself to your friends in this city during your last visit, and said that if the Capital was moved here, you would sell your land and abandon the city as your future home. Now, Mr. President, you should not have made that remark, nor should you entertain such a view of the Capital of your country. You are the official head of the American nation, and it becomes you to bear aloft the American name and the American character. It is unpatriotic, unstatesmanlike, to entertain such a view of the Capital of your country. I am aware that Washington City has given a bad experience, but I have shown you why. I have shown you that it was not the distinctive presence of the Capital that has given the bad experience to Washington, but the unfortunate relation of the representative power of the nation with the non-representative interests and civilization of the people. The mechanic, the merchant, the banker, the landlord, the laborer, and all are dependent upon Government patronage for subsistence; and no dependent people can live above demoralization. They will as surely generate vice and inefficiency as stagnant water generates malarious scum. The people of Washington City are chained to dependency; and the nation suffers by resting its arms on weakness. In fact, Mr. President, Washington City is unjustly dealt with by the United States Government by the control exercised over the people of that city. Under the policy of reconstruction, all have heard much about republican forms of government for the revolted States, and yet the District of Columbia, with a population greater than is contained by several of the States represented in Congress, has no political voice in the national councils. In this there is manifestly a wrong. The degradation of the people also carries with it the degradation of the national legislature. Congress is nothing but a national committee on streets and alleys for Washington City—an official capacity degrading to the official body it is. The removal of the Capital would benefit Washington and exalt the nation. It would place the people of the District of Columbia upon their own resources, and develop their smothered energies. It would give to the nation a new manifestation of life, consummate our national transition, and herald the inauguration of the NEW REPUBLIC.

The new Capital must be adjacent to one of our great metropolitan cities, where the people of the city will be as independent in their industry and interests as the Government itself. Then the relationship of the two independents will serve a common and benign influence for the welfare of both. The strong and representative elements and interests of civilization will unite, at the home of the Government, with the legislative and representative interests of the people for the common benefit of the entire nation. Then will experience reverse the conviction which you entertain, Mr. President, that the presence of the Capital would be injurious to any locality. Your position in this matter argues that the Capital should be abolished and the Government dissolved. Such should be the case if the Capital is a great national Pandora box. But, Mr. President, before it is established as a fact that the Capital of this country (for I think the people of no other nation argue it) will demoralize any locality where it may be placed, the people ought to test the validity of the charge with four years of experience with a President, a Cabinet, and a Congress, composed of men of a high type of intellectual statesmen, of pure morality, and an exemplary life-practice. You know, Mr. President, there is much in habit, much in the character of men, that affects society for good or evil. And, Oh, what a god-send to this nation it would be, if it could only be ruled and its laws made by the best and highest type of men. You must know how benign and elevating the influence of such men would be! You know " in that great argument which gave us the two most consummate orations of antiquity, the question was, whether Athens should grant Demosthenes a crown. He had fled from battle, and his counsels, though heroic, brought the city to ruin. His speech is the masterpiece

of all eloquence. Of the accusation by Æschines, it is praise
enough to say that it stands only second to that. In it Æschines
warns the Athenians that in granting crowns they judged themselves, and were forming the character of their children." Hear
his eloquent words: "Most of all, fellow-citizens, if your sons
ask whose example they shall imitate, what will you say? For
you know well it is not music, nor the gymnasium, nor the
schools, that mold young men, it is much more the public procla-
mations, the public example. If you take one whose life has no
high purpose, everybody who sees it is corrupted. Beware,
therefore, Athenians, remembering posterity will rejudge your
judgment, and that the character of a city is determined by the
character of the men it crowns." Mr. President, the people of
this nation ought to heed the lesson of Æschines and teach it in
the capital of their country.

## X.  IMMEDIATE REMOVAL DEMANDED.

Mr. President, having passed over the field of discussion and
presented to your mind an array of facts and arguments that are
positively incontestable by any man, and can only be ignored by
a stolid stupidity at variance with the genius of our national
progress and continental greatness, I now insist that the immediate removal of the National Capital is demanded; the facts, as
well as the enlightened judgment of the American people, decide
that Washington is unfit to be the national metropolis of our
Government; and the universal conviction that the removal of the
Capital is only a question of time, coupled with the fact that its
present removal would not, in any possible way, adversely affect
the general interest of the Government, but rather give it new
life, argues incontrovertibly the wisdom of taking immediate
steps for the removal to the grand Valley of the Mississippi.

Every day of delay, Mr. President, in taking positive initia-
tory steps for the removal, so much the more stints the Republic,
retards the great mission of our people in their peaceful conquest
of the Continent, and the complete organization of the Government into an imperial Republic of States. The mission of our
people is sublime. Why stand ye in the way? Why not move

with our progress? Let us celebrate our hundredth anniversary with a new Capital, and the inauguration of the New Republic, whose all-embracing rule shall be the new liberty which this nation has given to mankind. Let us go forward in our continental mission, carrying out the designs of Columbus and Humboldt, apostolic citizens of our destiny. Let us rise above everything sectional, personal, or local, and move forward in our national purpose to the peaceful conquest of the continent. Let us bind it with iron bands from ocean to ocean, and from the Lakes to the Gulf. Let us traverse it by steam to every part of its wide domain, and hasten the time when in every quarter it will be jeweled with flourishing towns and cities and the land everywhere be made to bloom by the industry of our people.

Let us raise ourselves up; let us rise to the grandeur of the conception of one vast continental Republic, yielding to one beneficent law, and which shall be adorned with its crowning honor—a continental Capital worthy the nation, the symbol of whose power it is—great in its character of the nation whose design it accomplishes—fixed in the center of the States—overlooking the nation—the nation itself the sovereign of its power, and the Capital a part of the nation—with peerless dome reaching the heavens, and around whose earthly splendor ages will revolve in obedience to eternity's command, and in unison with the revolutions of majesterial States, around one central moving heart.          Most respectfully,

L. U. REAVIS.

St. Louis, Mo., *January 1, 1871.*

# REMOVING THE CAPITAL.

[*From the New York Tribune, January 28, 1871.*]

We to-day accord a full hearing to those who seek a transfer of the Federal metropolis from the banks of the Potomac to those of the Mississippi. Mr. L. U. Reavis, who thus addresses President Grant on the subject, was an early and has been not only an earnest but an indefatigable champion of removal. He has worked more, and we judge to better purpose, than any of his allies; and the considerations which favor removal have never been more fully nor more cogently set forth than they are in the letter herewith published.

Yet we think the President is substantially if not technically right in his position that the Capital is not to be removed by a mere majority vote in each House—a majority which may number less than one-third of the members entitled to sit in that House. The Capital of a great nation is not to be mounted on wheels and dragged hither and thither as a casual majority may dictate. We do not dispute the legal efficacy of such a vote; we only maintain that removal is so grave a topic that, though the Constitution does not expressly prescribe it, something very like a Constitutional amendment should be required to effect it. And this is what the President intended by his casual remarks quoted by Mr. Reavis.

On the next point we are in full accord with Mr. Reavis. The Capital question should be fully considered and finally settled now. The westward and southward extension of our area, until it has become many times what it was in 1787, raises a fair presumption that the Capital needs to be re-located. The fact (if fact it be) that the Valley of the Potomac proffered the fittest site in 1800, by no means proves that it remains such to this day. The fair inference is otherwise. Hence we say, let us take up the subject and dispose of it conclusively—that is, for so long as our country shall remain essentially what it is. If we shall go on annexing until we rule the entire continent, it is probable that New Orleans, or Vera Cruz, or Nicaragua, or Panama, will then be the spot for our Capital. But, having quadrupled our original area by additions on two sides only, and there paused, let us determine whether Washington shall or shall not remain the Mecca of our office-seeking pilgrims, before we spend another mill in buying costly grounds and erecting buildings at Washington, which could not be sold for five per cent. of their cost in case the Government shall ever leave them behind it.

But we are not convinced that a central location is so important as Mr. Reavis esteems it. Other things being *quite* equal, such location is expedient; but other things rarely or never *are* equal. So London is the Capital of Great Britain, Paris of France, Stockholm of Sweden, and Lisbon of Portugal, though neither of them is in the center of the kingdom. Nay, St. Petersburg, the modern Capital of Russia, is by no means so central as was that Moscow which Peter the Great abandoned. Rome is not so near the center of Italy as Florence is; yet the latter is about to give place to the former. China is a very old, conservative country; yet Peking, her modern capital, is not so central to her territory as her earlier capitals were. In short, we concede to geographical position a very subordinate importance in the location of a seat of government. Mr. Reavis may wisely consider that his own St. Louis is not so near the center of our present domain as Topeka or Fort Riley, and govern himself accordingly.

We have not a doubt that New York is the most desirable point in the Union for the location of its Capital. Nine-tenths of our own people whose duties constrain them to reside or sojourn at the Capital, with ten-tenths of the old world's embassadors and other visitants, would decidedly prefer it. Art, literature, the drama, music, and everything that interests or delights mankind, are more abundantly and cheaply enjoyed here than elsewhere in the new world. Moreover, our politics and municipal rule are so thoroughly rotten that even the presence of Congress and the Federal departments could not further corrupt them.

Yet we do not ask nor seek a removal of the Capital to our city. We are quite content with Washington, though we are confident that one hundred million dollars would have been saved ere this by a location which afforded the denizens of the Federal metropolis somewhat to live on besides the Government. That the present location was a very grave mistake, we have long been convinced; and we are not sure that the blunder is beyond remedy. But read Mr. Reavis on this point, and form your own opinions.

www.ingramcontent.com/pod-product-compliance
Lightning Source LLC
Chambersburg PA
CBHW030912260626
47169CB00008B/2807